D1073973

The programmers of tomorrow are
the wizards of the future.

— Gabe Newell

If I Were A Wizard, published by Paul Hamilton, 2017.

ISBN: 978-0-646-97896-3

Cover design and layout by Simon Howe.

www.wizardcodingbook.com

If I were A Wizard

Written by Paul Hamilton
Illustrated by Simon Howe

My morning forest is filled with the energy of life. A baby kookaburra laughing wildly at the possibility of another exciting adventure. A mother ringtail possum scurrying up a tree, exhausted after a long night spent hunting for her family. The burning stare of a great horned owl, vigilantly monitoring every movement on the forest floor.

1

But if you concentrate, and you're quiet...
really, really quiet. Oh, and still...very, very
still. You may just hear a tiny voice. And
that would be Mrs. Furn, my teacher.

"OK class, what do you want to be when you grow up?"

3

"I want to be a professional football player", Henry confidently states.

"I want to be a doctor", announces Bonnie.

"I want to be an architect", says Milton.

Next, Mrs. Furn turns to me and asks, "What do you want to be when you grow up, Hazel?"

I think long and hard, and then I reply,

"I want to be a wizard!"

Mrs. Furn considers carefully before responding. She knows that a child's imagination is delicate, and should be encouraged in order to grow.

"OK Hazel, what would you do if you were a wizard?"

I stand up, and as I do, my stance instantly becomes stronger than before. The words come to me naturally, and quickly, as if someone has taken control of my mouth. I feel like a puppet being controlled by its master.

I begin.

If I were a wizard...

I would make ten perfect waves so that
Cousin Milo could surf by the waterfall.

q

If I were a wizard...

I would help my Grandpa Leo retrace his steps so that he could find his glasses.

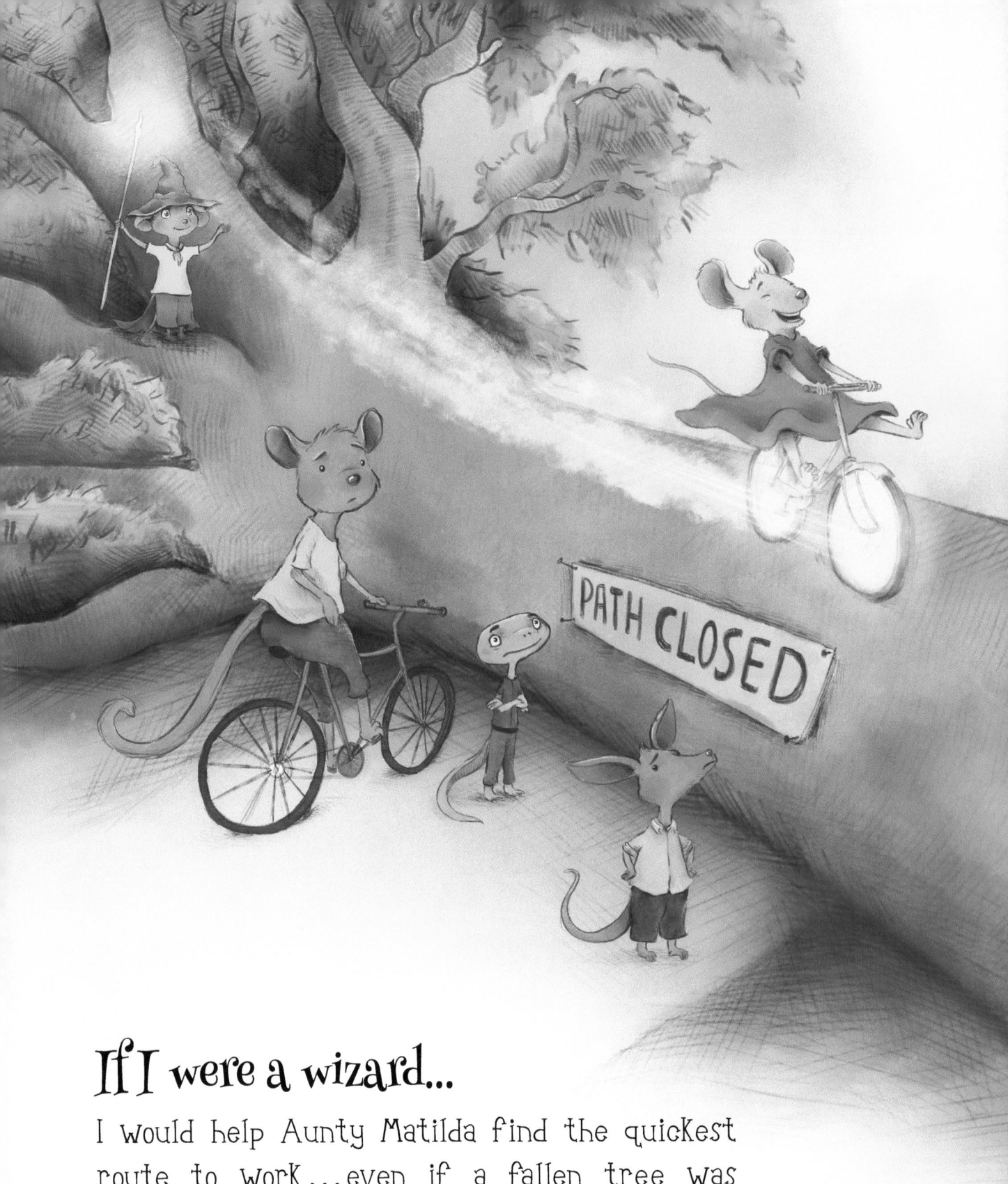

If I were a wizard...

I would help Aunty Matilda find the quickest route to work...even if a fallen tree was blocking the main path. She would never be late for work again!

If I were a wizard...

I would help Nanna Belle by labelling all of the containers in her pantry in big, clear letters. That way, she could easily find the ingredients needed to make my favourite cookies.

If I were a wizard...

I would help Great Grandma Sheila go check the mail each day...and I would remind her to take the umbrella with her if it was raining outside.

If I were a wizard...

I would help Dad learn all of the steps to creating a new meal...something besides Bug Bolognese!

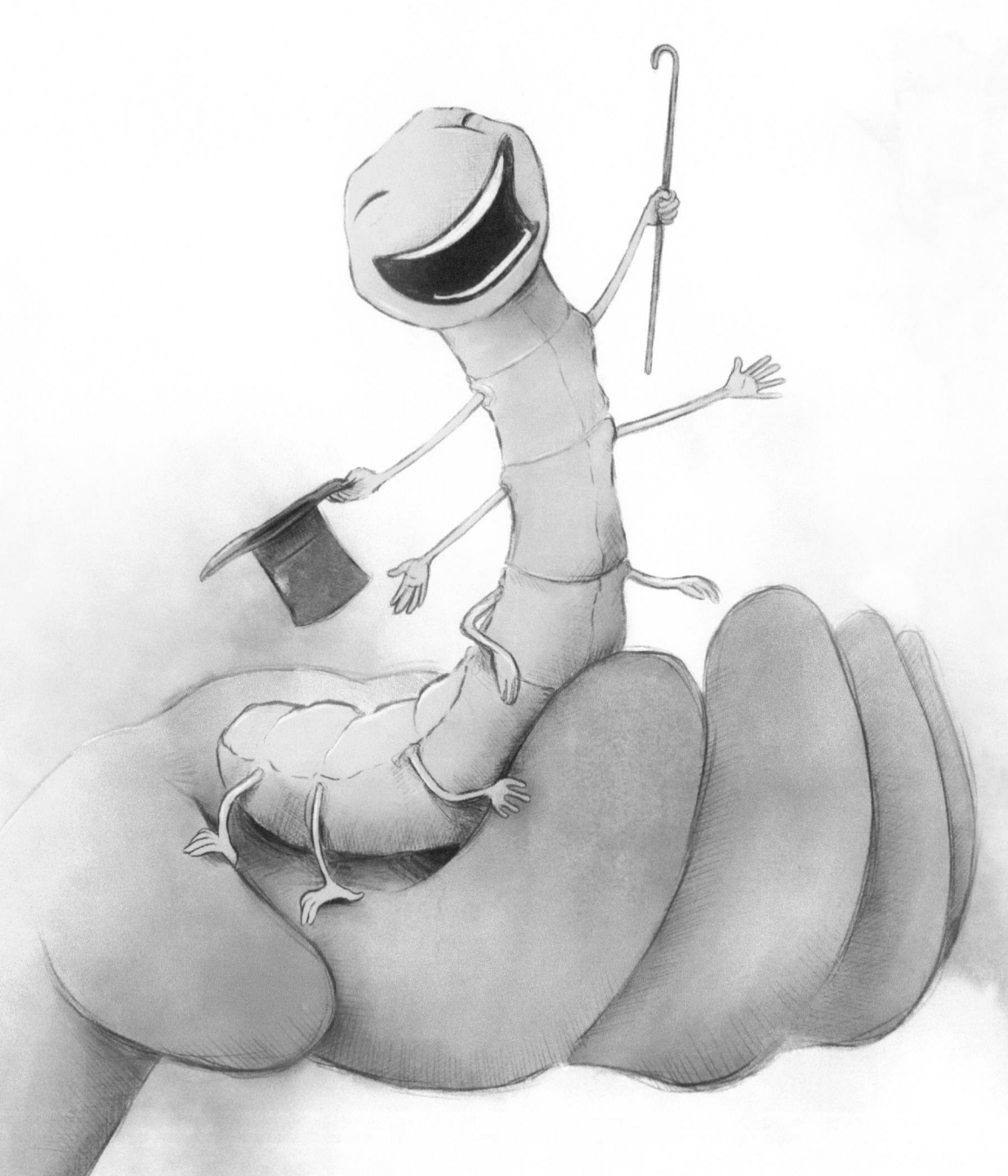

If I were a wizard...

I would teach my pet caterpillar Frank to sit, dance, and sing...all with a single hand command.

If I were a wizard...

I would find out exactly why Uncle Percy's car doesn't work, and I would fix the part that is not working.

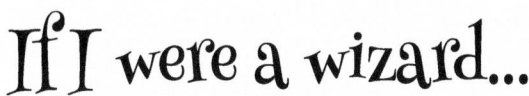

And, best of all,

If I were a wizard...

I would help people focus more on what they have in common so that we could solve all of the problems in the forest.

Mrs. Furn looks at me with a frustrated expression on her face, clearly wanting to move on with the lesson.

"But Hazel, wizards are not real!" she declares.

The lunchtime bell rings, and I scamper out the door with my computer under my arm.

The morning sun continues to rise over the forest canopy from the East.

As I run, Mrs. Furn's words play over and over in my mind. Suddenly, something inside me stirs, like a tiny spark that starts a flame. It's small, but it hits me hard. I smile and think to myself...

One day, I will
create magic!

Coding Concepts
Covered in This Book

Repeats and Loops

Page 9

Repeats and loops are ways of making things happen over and over again. Our wizard creates a perfect wave and then uses his magic to repeat the wave 10 times. What are some things that you spend a lot of time on that you would like to repeat?

Sequence and Order

Page 10

Have you ever lost something and had your parents tell you to "retrace your steps?" Sequence and order are important in coding because they make sure everything runs smoothly and happens in the correct order. Just imagine if we put on our pants before our underwear!

Algorithms

Page 11

An algorithm is a step-by-step set of instructions for completing a task. Aunty Matilda carries out all the steps to get to work, from opening the car door to arrival at work. There may be different steps and different routes to take - different algorithms. The most effective algorithm will get Aunty Matilda to work the fastest.

Variables

Page 12

Think of variables as labels. They are great ways of keeping track of things. Nanna would be helped by labels on the containers in the pantry. She would then know exactly which containers to grab in order to follow a recipe.

Conditionals

Page 13

When do you walk across a busy road? You walk if the walking sign is lit up, right? That walking sign is the condition. A conditional statement says if this happens, then something else should happen. Great Grandma needs to be reminded to take her umbrella with her to check the mail if it is raining.

Functions

Page 14

A function is where you group tasks. Every day, we perform simple tasks like collecting the mail and complex tasks like learning to prepare a new recipe.

Debugging

Page 16

Uncle Percy's car is broken. But is the entire car broken or simply a small part? Debugging code means finding and fixing errors in code. Very often, one small error stops a program from working. The trick is to act like a detective and find it!

Patterns

Page 17

Patterns exist everywhere. You will find them in mathematics, science, and literacy. They also occur in coding. Sometimes when we are problem solving and we remove all the differences - the things that are not important - we are left with solutions that we can use to solve problems.

Think of all the people in the world. What do we all need to survive? Maybe if we focus on the things we have in common and not on our differences, we could solve many of the world's problems.

About the Author

Paul Hamilton is a primary school teacher in Queensland, Australia. He is passionate about introducing students to coding concepts in a variety of ways, including through non-digital formats. Paul is a renowned, inspiring public speaker, and an advocate for the effective use of technology in schools. He's also an author and an app developer, who has been labelled by the Australian media - including The Age, The Sydney Morning Herald, and The Canberra Times - as a leading pioneer in the EdTech field.

Printed in the USA
CPSIA information can be obtained
at www.ICGtesting.com
LVHW070916020923
756749LV00022B/42